The Hat Rack Tree

Selected Poems from
theforestforthetrees, 1980-1993

Charles Stein

Station Hill

Published by Station Hill Literary Editions under the Institute for Publishing Arts, Barrytown, New York 12507, with grateful acknowledgement to the National Endowment for the Arts, a federal agency in Washington, D.C., and the New York State Council on the Arts, for partial financial support of this project.

Cover photograph by Charles Stein ©1994.
End Papers by Catherine Schieve ©1994.

ACKNOWLEDGEMENTS
I wish to express my warmest thanks to Don Byrd, who has, I think, heard every word almost as it sprung in "the forest"; and George Quasha, who read the manuscript at various stages and who has been a companion of the spirit for so many years; and to Susan Quasha for design; and to Anastasia McGhee and Vicki Hickman for help with typesetting. And to Megan Hastie with my love.

Many of these poems, in their present version or in prior variants, have appeared in: *Boundary 2, Conjunctions, Credences, The Equinox, Hambone, Io 41 (Being=Space × Action), Nadir, O.ars, Sulphur, Under a Single Moon,* the privately circulated texts: *Four Before the Forest, The Sad World, The Holy Mountain,* and a tape: *from theforestforthetrees* published by Chris Mason.

Library of Congress Cataloging-in-Publication Data

Stein, Charles, 1944-
    The hat rack tree : selected poems from Theforestforthetrees,
1980-1993 / Charles Stein.
      p.   cm.
    ISBN 0-88268-180-X : $9.95
    I. Title
PS3569.T363H37   1994
811'.54--dc20   94-747
                                     CIP

Manufactured in the United States of America.

CONTENTS

Note on *theforestforthetrees* 2

The Lions 3

Pages from *First Forest* 11

The Null Credential 22

A Parmenides Machine 25

Being Mice 30

The Sad Machines 42

The Power of Silence 52

Five Nails 60

Two Dreams 74

Song 76

First Message 77

Song 78

Second Message 79

The Tower 80

Entity 82

The Bachhoe 83

Later Poems from "The Sad World" 86

Concordance 97

The Hoopoe 102

They Take the Car Away 107

The Hat Rack Tree 110

Notes 113

NOTE ON *theforestforthetrees*

theforestforthetrees is a textual practice, not a single long poem. It includes all the writing in poetry I have done since the early 80s. To date it amounts to several shelves of folders, binders, and notebooks. I write freely and compose from this work pieces and compilations of pieces when occasions for publication arise. I hope the name suggests that the whole of it cannot be surveyed but exists solely for the sake of the particular moments of writing it affords and for the particular compilations. Yet each poem or collection does emerge from a "forest" of writing activities that in some way informs them all.

The Hat Rack Tree

The Lions

for Lou Kleinsmith

In the kingdom of the bowels that is language . . .

the animal
chasing itself

nature consuming nature

"serpents that eat the darkness

out of the burning stones"

◆

as if for sure I had been there . . .

Not true.   I have.   And am.

small sounds rising from themselves . . .

the last blue cornflowers of October . . .

◆

The kindness and concern it has —
to relinquish all projection of itself
if only called back to its own.

The intricate fictions desire their own surcease

when faced with The Lake.

There are continuous gradations of enclosure but truly . . .

as if this sudden silent rock of moon

had many names

♦

That which stands against
continuous with its distance from the eye
in the light of further inquiry.

Dictum: language

including both whereof it speaks

space, dense with responsibility

head full of stones

♦

In the turbidity
yet it grows.
So events of the day
are shadows too
and the figures which arrive in many dreams —
events with their own pertinacity,
not just that they *produce* . . .

♦

In every coming forth
what goes away,
opposite but not equal, probably more . . .

The woman in the many photographs
with the false name

the transformations manifest in "life"

4

the colored force
becomes a slightly different
colored force

the gentle surface of an infinite sphere

alone in the soiledness

the tawdry racks

◆

If some "it"

is "there"

we never get there.

Nobody standing
under the rain of living apples

the little bells
correlate the falling Yods . . .

The lions resolve to live apart from lions.

They are a pride
of lions

before they are themselves, autonomous,

even granting a more than conventional regalism to *each*

in his collective "what" . . .

And if that "it"

is just some "what" —

◆

I am as stars
or snow

walking in back of the universe
surely there must be some elephant
certainly a cow
among the monuments
at the bottom of the breath
the blackness of night and the stars of night
reach
into the thickness and the things
plummeting the still morass
a doubling back
"AUM"
to neutralize
"Maaaaaa"

◆

     curious wavering
         over a surface of water
            in a quieting bowl
the broken leaves and other autumnal debris
swirl with inertial particularity
       and come to rest

      absolute sadness accumulating its need of dead
the ancient halls
       accumulate the figures from our own
          cohabitations with them
               being in the world

◆

He is accumulated into the presence of himself.
His eternal Ka
discoursing with the others
in a night of grief.

◆

The movement to make it more
succeeds
abandoning itself
until what remains alone is that which was
to be attained
and the motion though swift and sure
proceeds from a certain propulsion
less than minimal.

◆

Slow
          as stars
                    appear

     in this very body

                    the unstable majesty

               no need to tell
               but in the need to tell

                              gold of no gold

◆

The covert-overt
reverses the cover

and all there is
gathers in just this one
selecting it
from multiple facets of it
releasing the subject
in a vastness of noises
which are quiet in totality
buy yield these small
illusionary pips
one by one

♦

Becomes himself
and loses himself

releases the fundamental
from its walking and its plunder
and thus releases the plundered
fellows of its wandering
into the simultaneous and alone
from which they come —

the single eaglets
in the chalky boughs

the rapid mouse
and its path between big reed bulbs

dots on earthy tablets

rocks in the hills

that same old dog alone along the roadway

the naked shirt
wagging at the lions

the lions
seated on the porch
with loose and golden boney shoulders pointing
across the reeds
to the hills

the broken hills
rounded, then cut, a flat table
at the top of them
rough and grey

the one huge mountain

the green sky

◆

Walking all that distance
for incredible numbers of years
three Buddhist Aeons
towards the water

pointing to it
seeing a barge
across the horizon
with a cloud-like skull
floating over the flatness
and the slowness
and the motion
of the barge
heavy yet afloat
across the water

already there
yet walking
to meet himself

grasping himself beforehand in a bizarre
concordance of pictures
before the mind

a dog
        walking nervously
becomes a lion
        walking deliberately
an elephant
        walking solemnly
becomes a boy
on a beach

whale hulks ride in from the foam
and the most difficult thing about them is the stench
of death by water

the bones become language itself
unanimously arching over humanity

taking all of us up in its collosal superstructure
confounding our being in its intricate hypotaxis
floating up ominously
it is impossible to tell just what keeps it afloat
lifting each in its levity
the strange sun setting in the west beyond the water
rises
because we approach it at such speed
it is a lion
and it opens its fiery mouth
a black dot growing huge at the center of the sun
inhaling the fumes of whales
on the isle below
safe
for a stay

we are deposited

Pages from *First Forest*

1

If independent mind achieve its ultimate,
what need then for petty self-assertion?

> Give your life away —
> every impulse and smart,
> open the lowest hell of who you are —
> the doors in the walls of the abdomen,
> the windows in the spine . . .

The magistrate has longed to become a fish,
perhaps because he has not jumped in water since a boy.

Big lakes of autumn water draw the magistrate
as he wanders in his fevered fantasy
out of public office to the woods.
He sees the colors still in the lake depths
and subtle mists
that pass across
from bobbing dock to distant rocky beach and shadow tree.
He calculates his nature,
drops his formal costume on a limb
and settles in
             to the gentle water.
A pickerel speaks to him.
Arrangements are constructed.
A beast with human trunk and head of fish
instructs him in the wisdom of
the mountain water deeps
and rules of life therein . . .

2

(not willing to do it
 or
  yet
 to
  have
 done with
 having to do it)

        the goddess
         sat
          on her throne
           with fingers clenched

                    ◆

I flew so fast
the fields of force
that held my atoms together
fell behind the motion

        I looked in the mirror
                but I wasn't there

        (all things
                a mirror)

I moved towards the still horizon
but never drew near

                    ◆

3

The river became
indecipherable:

a snake
and then a bull

and bit
dust

and lost its horn

◆

I don't notice
clothes. Consider it
shallow habit
to notice
clothes.

How have people
come to be
as they are?

(As every thought
has entered the mind
it knows.)

— sirens in the alley
getting used to the city —

loud people in the room behind the wall

He comes in here, plays with the machines, the radios.

The woman waits on the corner for the
same bus I am waiting
on the corner for the bus
for

Now at the end of the counter the fellow
leans yapping to a woman with boots who's
just about to be going to get up and leave now.

She doesn't like to go on hearing
the heavy duty yapping
of the fellow.

Many people are quite crazy
because of the "dips."

Somebody very well accoutred actually
getting off the phone
makes faces
opening his mouth to stretch obscure
neck tendons.

What is very important —
myths miss it too.

     But we have to have these great
old stories, haven't we?
Horrible shirts
         storming all over the mountains
         uprooting hulks of trees

Get him out of here!

        "You win the argument
           but I'll beat the crap out of you
              anyway"
                   essentially

The kinds of poetry
      we pretend
   we are not writing
            in order to distend
      some other
            kind
      of writing

Oak club
         with which I bonked
                           the famous pig

      Sorry feelings
      want
      reality to be
      another way
      Oh Please
      don't get all humped up

Deeper depth of doing what one has or is
doing. Pissed
because of muffler dent.
The state should pay.
All the people coming
into this restaurant tonight
are ugly repulsive distorts.
I want coffee.
My mood is changed.
Can't get mind around
it. Need to plug
and bend some.
Give me money.
Get me out of here!
Pristine WHAT?
Just sitting and wishing
to get more wits. Hope
friends are going to walk
in that door. He burnt

his hand
on Nice Hot Rolls.
I'm different.
Suffer because of it.
Feel sort of queer
and lonely. Going
to get up and go
home now. That old woman
now affronts
the room, bearing up
nobly. The rest
of the universe converted by
the very cheerfulness
of her attitude
into the burden she carries.

Dumpy people sit together.

Some dumpy people
            used to be the rich ones.

And some
are rich ones
still.

Bank nets can't think
and yet those bank nets know —

wonderful pools
or parks
in ancient kingdoms

Having to remember details and pursue 100%

. . . pools
in civil grots
where beautiful women are changed
deeply and become

lotus pods
that bleed when
other women
pluck them

and the earth grew bark
about her feet
and only a weeping
token of her loveliness
remains
> *as a face*
> *on a stalk*

4

How can I leave you be in me —
> myths to leap inside of —
psyche's appetite, soul's mouth
> > **bound to rock**
> > **with monster**
> **surging from the brine all slurp and snout?**

Do people have sex in **their bodies?**

People eat nuts and **screws**
> but don't know why
doctors aver.

You can't say that —
it's late!
> Please wait
to be seated.

I walk
> into the place
> > and plunk
my baggage
down.

The concierge is abused by my bumptious deed.

I want to be sweet
but ugly surly habits moil my attitude.

What's happening?

My wife
        is mixing
                with the town.

They bring you coffee but forget the spoon,
fill the cup too high so the milk won't fit.
It dribbles o'er the lip and threatens my papers.

This bad music is not
        exactly
          only
bad music. It is
          bad music
                  too . . .

Just which side of the mirror are you on?

Two people talking in loud objectionable
manner at the back of the bus.

Always something
        realer than we are.

This Great Enlightenment? In what does it obtain?
Little rocks that talk, have patience, and are loved.

◆

You look better than I do
but the cops are after *you*
for hopping rails.

Subpoena.
You know what subpoena means —

The smart criminals now are taking courses.

I got my nice pipe back today
but the stem doesn't bend
    correctly any more.

Quiet now. The mirror fogs and clears.
Indecipherable faces. They come from anywhere
into the same
        place.

5

What kind of notions are we?

Sacked urbanities, mule team
drives
across counties
governed by enormity

        you can't get out of your house or have   your house
because there are no places
                without a map
                        to spot them in

            he flimps her fingers
            but she doesn't care

mere "flatus vocis"

      I am a molecule or globule, frankly
a random fluctuation of constituent elephants
        in compensation for the absence of a world

Whatever happens — must
Whatever doesn't — can't

False.

My most intelligent friends appear to be
constant misconstructions of each other.

Flight over shifting wibbits of sound plan

river mastiness

[some of these words are real words but untrue
while other, unreal words, promulgate verities]

syzygys

they cannot be measured
because they do not exist

in order to articulate just what we think we know
it is certain we must become
almost inarticulate in our willingness to remove

otiose lexical items
laden with thought
rife from another time
no longer applicable

Wizzards I think, but no longer wise

the kinds of hats these thinkers
have to wear

as if the secret darkness that subtends
the ambience of Enlightenment
placed in oneself a reality so unimaginable
it takes a strong mind to bumble in
among the fox-like being forms
quibbling with the debits of nonentity

to make a space
                the size of an unendurable instant
last so long.

                You choose one option and the others go off
in their own worlds —

                do they greet you later
                on the other side of mortality
                to mock you in your adventitious
                                predilection for the actual?

A car slews
and dashes through
the snowy trees.

Slumped in the driver seat   surrender everything.

6
                elephants freely choosing
                        their future orbits

a curious feature of the physical world
        that there are no features
                that there is no
world . . .

                I become a serious person
                believing the book I read

                what hasn't happened
                leaves us room to think

                unreal but not impossible
                fellows with curious hats

                askance in the twilight

The Null Credential

"You know I don't understand poetry"
my grandmother used to say
when I would torture her
with the writings I'd produced that day.

People think it something difficult, you have
to know how to like it, or to understand

rather than   *impossible*   the amber
light of the creature's eyes   the size of *bushels*

departing from the place in which they
at the same time remained, exhausting
you (the zealot) who wished to peer
into the Holy Regions without "credential"

proof that you too had been exhumed, that a spark
from your soul belonged to such
supernal treasure troves of light

that the circular activity of the thought in your own mind
should not consume you as you dive
for the very center of its coursing
and it become a flaming sword to measure
and abate curiosity, stem desire,
cut back undeveloped ego lust or sad,
insatiable, long pursuit of power

That the eyes of the Living Beasts were huge as "bushels"

(bushes   inside of which the power
to cognize and to remonstrate lay hidden

And the speech in your own mind, if pure
— a pure glass reflecting
everything and allowing
you to pass
into the chamber of the Throne

And no One
on it

Sky so lustrous with stars   that walking were possible
by its light alone while

untamed horses wander on both
sides of the all-night highway

And as I remove   garment after garment
I discover that the Institutions and Establishments
of reality are nothing at all but the
correlatives of the garments themselves
and that the qualifications, the purities, are nothing
but the "null credential"
that one be capable of giving all away
without remorse, without confusion, without shame
before the assignations of the Angels of The Face, Gate
Keepers, Archons, Guardians, or whatever who
without your "showing" this null credential   everywhere
demand of you
tokens of performances you shall not
by any means
produce

But the animals
                    multiply
        their outlook
                    before your very gaze

    going forth and coming
    back into place
                    being
    the movement of your own thought at that moment

    whether turbid or aroused
    by terror, or by amazement,
    stunned

But willing to remove
the garment of each long-committed
act of intellection . . .

A Parmenides Machine

It is as old as it thinks itself to be.

It is as old as itself. Its old self.

And in being just that old
it goes on growing older —

older than it has been until now,
older than it is now . . .

The young shoot grows
on the trunk of the ancient oak
though older now.

Its youth self is retained
as that which it has been
and, as, older now, it throws its youth aside —
that youth self comes into being
as just the youth it was
now
for the first time.

    I feel the wind
blow across the water
just enough to cause the sails to move.

There are people on the beach now
in the summer
now that it is winter.

The music is strutting backwards.

He plays the improvisation
sitting sideways. Scratching the phrases
across the keys in a rapid jitter
that fits the notes
aptly to the measure
and yet I feel the music strutting sideways.

We ourselves are beginning to get up and move
in an awkward manner
away from the deck and the deck chairs.

It is impossible to see us moving
and yet we are picking up our hats
and walking off to the right
under the shadow of the veranda
and going into the lounge to purchase a beverage.

We ourselves are beginning to get up and move
in a curious manner.

It is impossible to see us do this, impossible to stir
the memory of it,
but we do it — we have done it —
and as we pass the scene in a sail boat
our having done it
in just this jittery manner
      moving aslant
            looking askance

and walking quietly
under the shade of the veranda

comes into view.

Coming into being comes into view.

The whole comes into being
as the future idles on.

It wasn't there before at all.

Our youth was not our youth
until the ancient priest-thinker
arrived with his oaks
propped up on a hobbled machine.

The noises that it makes in that intolerable sun blaze.

His white beard flows like the sun blaze.

We ourselves are walking to the right
having crossed the line
on the floorboards of the sun deck
where the shadow of the veranda
crosses in the noon hour.

White splotches of sunlight
and dark and sharply outlined patches of shadow
cross our bodies —
                    the line of division
twixt shadow and sun blaze
moves across our bodies as we move
across the deck
to go into the lounge.

How old are you
these days.

Your youth comes into being as you grow old.

The aged priest-thinker,
hobbling into the sun blaze of his agedness
appears as in his youth to put the questions
before the ancient machine — thus to become
young again
and for the first time.

He is old and young in a single figure
and the shadow of the veranda
crosses his body at noon
and does not move
as the river of questions streams across his memory.

It is impossible to say in what direction we seemed
                              to be moving just then.

Perhaps it was to the right of the shadowed deck chairs
and away from the sun-blanched water
towards the veranda.

The elderly priest-thinker
was serving drinks and behaving
in a jittery manner
as the shadow of the boat deck
passed magisterially across the window glass.

The music seemed to have been getting louder.

He complained of his age.

The questions were sputtering
out of the ancient mechanism.

There was a certain strain inside him
as if he had run this course before
in his youth
and that that youth had now to be summoned
before the small but particular company
perfectly suited to attend the mechanism.

The others complained of his age.

He said he was an ancient horse chariot driver
required to go the journey
to the northernmost stars
one more time
before he regained his youth again —
that this was the method, the machinery
by which one, starting in the same place,
distinguishes figures in that locality
coming into being
as if for the first and only time. And only now.

Being Mice

1

in the middle of the music   (meaning

                                  this little patch of time I
                                     happen to pass by in

                Imagine a space vehicle   manned by Name Alone

I have forgotten the number they gave me
and now my name becomes vague to me

I try to catch it as it passes
in a costly limousine

The clothes I wear won't give me away —
the voices I muster to speak to the master . . .

2

           These people are cats
at the door   all   summer
                     seeking
status   among the   other
cats that
         LIVE here   cats that
know   that   they belong

                   and the evening
sky's   hay colored   light
glowed in the sheep's coat

3

In a party of friends and acquaintances
suddenly a small
cat comes
close to me and
starts to speak.

It says that I
have been mistaken

about its nature.

Of *course* cats speak.

I try to tell everyone
but obstructions
block our conversation.

♦

A long necked cat accuses me.

There is scratching and cat meowls
of a violent and distressing kind:

cats attacking human throats!

I am a Cat Killer
and one of the worst!

(People will know I am crazy
but there's no escape
from cats'
howling, scratching
and speaking in terrible whispers
                              all night
                                        everywhere

4

The sound "ite" as in "bite"
now.

Bite now.

◆

I threw the black crow claw away, hating evil —
not even wanting
to possess the tainted object

And therefore request
a settlement regarding
the lexical item "BEYOND" viz:

That posit that acts as a gland
to secrete our secrets.

"Beyond the nature of the giraffe
a beast with just that nature
lopes towards sundown."

"Beyond the causes that conspired to bring us here
a living monument to its own exclusion
flames at the heart of the day."

And no boat exists

to skim the quiet harbor surface long enough

to skim the quiet harbor surface long enough

I have good teeth.

They shine

like Mice.

Giant Noises

hide in the Toad's Sky

5

That
dog
is
at
least
one
half not
dog

6

That
Ape
men thought
to talk
sign talk to

thought him-
self a
man to
talk to

7

The cat at the top of the stairs has
a serious look in his loungey eyes as
I climb the stairs and confute him.

8

My hat had vanished.

When that cat that
sat up looked straight at it,

that hat had had it.

9

Moments of mind reflected in moments of language
scorching white paper —

"The Language of Lights"
and the world.

(Your reading so massive so curious —

      white doves spring from your hands)

And did I detect a tremor in the voice of the wise one who whis-
                                      pered:

      "It does not die" ?

The dark halls
pure as space

horses

      marching across Paradise

and the marks left by their hooves in the muddy turf
were "read" by the sages of that area

    And we stood by
    and we cyphered
    and we watched the vivid creatures
    cross and cross again

and our pleasures passed   into the manifest universe

10

I wanted to attempt
           "fresh textualities"
                       even to let go

long enough to arouse
the flaming letters
along the perforations
wearing clothes of the wrong sex
being a tiger
in one penetration and being
mice
       later
               skating across the balcony
first I was just you
                   walking
           backwards
                       somewhere

   very hot. The city of Corinth does not
exist exactly. Nor Thebes. Blank trees
in the areas designated by those names these days.

It was impossible to retain the use of the car.

I was ill until fresh passengers relieved discourse.

The place I retain in your heart is small consolation
for the loss of essential services.

The margins of our thought had just been shifted
that much further onward towards oblivion . . .

11

"The Cat Forgives Its Phenomena"

The light goes off
            but the cat remains.

I lose
      my place
             in my mind
                      and a light goes on

      at the edge of the botched mentation
      such that   at last   I can see
                                      straight
             into the world:

             Sunlight
             shining
             on water

             people swimming in the pond

Savage Beetles Sail Across The Dunes

12

All the things that cross the mind — don't think of these.

And all the things we feel and wish to do
even in a few moments from now
after this brief exercise has come
to its allotted terminus
and the world goes on —

And all the associative links we know —

don't link them now.

That mind I own
deep in the sockets of the skull bones —
the thoughts that think themselves
running amock in those sockets

trying to shake loose of the effort
to achieve a paramount stance —

an exercise so intimate and obtuse
to the local chatter that
it rides on Nothingness alone!

(thinking the mind

is not the mind

but somebody else . . .

13

An Ideal Object

produced before

the world.

A look

coming out of a head

and a bird

shooting across space

interrupting that look —

(An *entire life* has just gone by)

In front of a large audience

the magician does

a truly impossible

thing:

He produces an Ideal Object

before the world.

14

Does logic
compel
the thought it owns?

No.

We
compel
each thought.

And who are we?

Since

the world

began.

15

And now The Vessels break
and ruby juices splash on the tiles.
A crowd with tapers makes the midnight crossing.

The giantess and her consort, stashed beneath bed rock,
trying to become an obstacle ignored till now.

16

I am taken
for the power
I desire

(people think I'm *real*.

I am not real.

I stand on the roof.

I vanish.

I see
 the sleeves
  of my selves
   grow dim on the plane.

17

An old hotel
my house had been
I happen to be
living in
  on
the banks
of what used to be
a river . . .

This piece of paper

goes on forever . . .

The Sad Machines

Part One

1

The machines that have been established, old or not old
. . . having to break them.

And the parts
lie out
on the plain.

And false blueprints — erratic diagrams
that
somebody brings up from a state to the south
deploy deep contradictions.

And the reason people do this —
the reason people stay up late to destroy the large machines
taking pains to scramble   the apparatus-map-objects . . .

2

Someone is riding in on a new car.

A mirror is set in her belly.

I can hear the heat   her soul emits   lounging next to me.

It is an impossible sensation.

I can feel the heat   taking place inside her body.

This is exactly what I mean.

3

Now other people come out of the dark
having something to emit.

Luminous blots
that do not take place in the material universe as such
therefore
nothing is disrupted in thought when we see them ride
through the room with no hinges — they pass through doors.

How immensely unserious of these beings to evade
solidity of night objects —
they seem not to know where they are.
They behave in a manner that betrays an incompetence to deal
     appropriately *at all* with conditions we find normal here
but where have *we* come from
and what is this blue caboose
that does not move — people keep it as a kind
and quaint museum.
Only inside — black water puddles.

The luminous blots are sentient creatures that's true
but the things they are aware of   are things from a blotted world.
They are out. They are blotted out.
But exude a casual light
so that if we have to assign to them a nature
it is a contradicted nature.
A nature blotted out.

When people emit these blots or are these blots
it sounds a lot like the sound   of apparatus-maps
disrupting huge machines.

4

The aged king   walks across the boat deck.

I ride the back of an elephant
and turn into a chinese
locality.

It is dark
and here and there vast
burnt-up boards
drop in the rubble
and a frantic barn owner balances on the beams
before they fall
against the darkness
of the house on fire.
And an octopus has died
and cast up its hulk on the sea surface
and later I think about a little corn man
about to be reborn.

5

The black table cloth where all cows are all nights long
as large as the lake.

Black Lake.

Something inside the being-body
flat and still
absorbing waves of heat or beams of light.

At the belly bottom
inside the mountain
there is some vast cave space
at the bottom of which a lake is black

44

just because no light gets in there.
It is a lake deprived
of lake light
and a lake so deprived   can have different events in it than
        brightly lighted lakes.

When wind or sunlight ruffles the tops of these
it makes the people who gaze at them very old.

But Black Lake is not old not young not good not bad.

It takes on no identities, new or old.

New or young.

Young or old.

But Black Lake had a key of many keys

dropped down into it from the top of a cavern

once

and once again twice I drop an old key
forever into the water in the darkness
where no body has ever been yet a key
hangs from the top of the cavern

and there is a moment at the center of a certain history

wherein that key drops down

breaking the water.

6

On the backs of elephants dozens of me glare
into the distant area
forgetful of being.

Fools are jigging on the top of a blue caboose
as the train goes by.

The train goes by itself.

Luminous noises
have the texture of whispers —
the whispers of giant beings
voiceless, though loud.

It is a train   fifty feet high   with the head of a dog.

7

So the people who emit and the faulty apparatus-map-objects
seem as one.
                    And sometimes they combine
like kings on the backs of elephants
triumphal through the towns

to persuade the local awestruck populations
about their awesome deep triangulations
emitting broken machines from the back of the sky.

The queen goes into the lake.
The old and local magistrate
takes off his fish-head —
takes off his riverine nostalgia,
does his public duty,
dons his robes,
starts to think and promulgate his wisdom
across the network of little rural towns
like a decent person.

Part Two

1

Every moment possesses a two-headed mammal.

Two little mice
run out of the body.

The whole replaces itself with another mouse hole
into the night of its own perturbation.

One of the mice has a large brown wooden spoon it found.

It took that spoon and dropped it into time
causing quite a pother.

The two-headed mouse disappears in its own attempt
to catch a glimpse of itself.
One thing looks in back of itself and one thing

looks ahead of itself and what it sees is another
version of itself
looking back at itself.

The aged king grows young again —
walks on the deck of the yacht in the sunlit bay.

At the moment when the sun goes down
the glitter on the ridge poles
unites with the silence of my mind
to open the earth for me.

Still-shots of myself thinking
in numerous poses
at many ages of my life
some not lived yet.

2

I stand on the backs of giants

and upside down suspended
from the enormous cavern
feeling that overwhelms me
are thousands more of me
suspended.

An infinite line of elephants
connected trunk to tail

and on the back of each of them
one of me.

One swart king sits
in his cabana
on top of each of the pachiderms
connected trunk to tail
proceeding
past a check-point
designated "now."

3

Part of it had once been a man.

It lay there   in the corner of the hut.

The creature was human except for the eyes —

    (sockets full of amber)

He was walking beside me and I turned to my left.
There was a curdling in the space
and then he was gone. I mean

he folded up inside his own concavity.

The cave that was in him   consumed him.

4

Spaces are of three kinds: they are acids,
bases or neuters. The acids actively seek
to dissolve the substance of the egg. The bases
seek to draw the substance in the egg out from it.
And the neuter space allows the egg to determine its own destiny
projecting its inner substance or withdrawing it,
according to circumstance and nature.

The blackness of the interior of the cave
became the luminosity of the egg surface.
The concavity
became the convexity.

Actuality became conceptuality.
The thing I thought, extended in time.
Time had two parts in each part.
It was a mammal
and the mammal had two heads.
And one of the heads passed a word to the ear of the other,
then vanished or seemed to lose material presence.
But the second head remained
and in front of it a third head sprang out
from the shoulders of the mammal.

At first the new head seemed a ghostly shape
but as the hard head turned toward it
this third one grew substantial
and inclined the ear it had
to the mouth of the other
the mouth of the other
delivered its word to the ear
of the third head
and then vanished
or seemed to lose materiality
while the third head turned away
and a fourth head sprang from the shoulder
without materiality at first

only a lucent blot
but then it turned
and began to assume physical existence
as it received the word
and the third head vanished
or seemed to lose materiality
while the fourth head turned away

conceptuality became actuality
and the time I spent was born in thought
and the mammal gave birth to two mammals
and the two mammals were the first beast and a new one
which grew out of it
and the two were one
and they spoke together
and the thing they said was a new thing
and the two mammals together and the new thing the two
        mammals spoke of
became one
and the mammals were one thing and the thing said another
and these two were one
and these two things as one thing was one thing
and these two things as two things was another thing
and these together made a new pair of two things

5

Inside the body of the mammal there is a cave
and when the mammals speak the cave becomes an egg
and the inside of the cave which was black
becomes the egg shell which is buff or white or blue
but always luminous, always pulsing, always sending waves.

The Power of Silence

"I don't *believe* in birds."

These books ARE birds.

But which birds.

Those that fly in a straggling V shape over the town

          (don't say which town)

Don't believe in them.

Things have actually to be true to be
                declared so, truthfully.

And anything at all   declares itself.

The talking people
  (forget about what they say)

    still say 'talking people' —

Silent knowledge.

The blue caboose goes by . . .

Which is it?

      The other person?

Or is it the spirit?

Something   we have all

    somehow got to get linked on to . . .

       What's wrong

with me?   I mean the REAL

me, the REAL

wrong. Not the thing I used to worry all the

time about. {{still do}}

"Some unknown factor

awesome because of its simplicity

that is determining our fate"

What place is this that the sayings
  possibly have no sense at all?

False. Moving through air. Able to read

words upon these pages

with the very sensitive bottoms

of their sensors,
they know English very well —

the whole system

and some of the things they
pick up   conform
    quite well
    to the rules they've learned —

The freedom to rule
lives
and go on and on
without knowing the limit
for the trip
up into the dynamite
caves
to seek the loosenings

We [a calendar. And on it
    days marked
    out in
    a boring way

someone's head
  is turning into an elegant
    string pattern

    bald   no ears

you look away

at what? We [

Someone is tracing its pattern
  in our business —
    fidgeting,   going back
  and forth across earth
  a small distance
      but again
          again
          and again

  between two cities
      or between home
  in a house
      and town

[going to the closet to stuff away something]

going on a hunt
in the middle of the night
stalking something
stalking oneself
being oneself but being
      unable to find oneself

so taking some thing one likes
and going out
into the balmy atmosphere of the city alone
in order to twin some object
reticent with destiny
to call one's own
by

A man
with the head of a fish
and only one eye

he was as big as a door
he kept us all as hostages
hostages for what though?

and he was always
        angry
            ironical
                and courteous
        he hated us
or needed to seem so

it was real enough
but *how* it seemed
shifted so quickly
estimation were radically
humbled
beyond recall

Though of course I don't fall
under the type
I am also
everybody
and must try out
all the marks
that happen to appeal to me
in order to complete my
                special view

If you move your point a great amount
you could perhaps become a
large horse or another
beast or a train
in the dawn
with boxcars but if you move
it only a small amount you become
another kind of person fat
if you aren't   taller if
you are tall

They keep changing
how old you are
right in front of your face
outside two people
you think are themselves —
disappear too slowly for that

The monster likes one of us.
Which? Not to destroy but to use
for purposes we can't understand
exactly but we do
his bidding with an attitude
anyway

the whole world
   that monster — how
 things (according to us)

   are

      forcing
       the matter
         of our lives

Now you are his slave   [stove].
You can never leave the house.
There is no way to outsmart an Unknown Intelligence.
Stay put and listen.

And the proof is spaces existent between us
and in them
things
that are not strings
not strung on lines like beads
but people   whose heads
are dogs   or gods
who mean things
coming and going
out
   by radiant design
themselves the products
of their own content
whose bodies are signs
   of the news they carry
they are coming from everywhere
   they are moving like heat
rising from the street
in the middle of the night
without hurry
   doing the bidding of their
inmost alarm
   and returning
to cities   whose avenues
                        whose exchanges
                                    whose patrols
elaborate   identities

   ◆

"An alien system of memory had invaded me."

Or no. It was my own.

Or I had changed my CHORDS
that I might now insert
myself   into what
hitherto had been another's narrative.

You are seated where you are
        or walking
    or lying in an unclean room
or in an office
  with brown chairs
or in a shop
  under the steady gleam
or in a barren place
  avoiding the janitors
or under the pressure of passionate circumstances

You are standing
  on the edge
    of a high cliff
    overlooking an interesting valley where a river
hidden by the forest
    nevertheless displays
      the structure of its meandering
          through low hills

            out   to another world

Five Nails

One: Air

It is quiet on the beaches.

There is no one around. And the sounds
of the breeze and the waves
are as no sound now. No one to hear them.

But soon a person comes to enjoy the silence.
And then the sounds begin.

Someone is sitting there
absorbed in the sound
of the surf as that sound rolls
wild across the dunes.

And soon the wind begins to blow from over the water.

First it disturbs the gulls that stand on the wharfs.
Then the wharfs themselves begin to become
disturbed from the strength the wind is developing.
Little by little the wind
makes a larger sound
and increases the menace.

The garments of the person
seated on the strand
flutter in the gathering wind.

Now all is a tumult of sand and sound, water and air
aswirl in an enormous turbulence. The person
remains
as long as that is possible. But soon this person too
flies up on the wind.

It blows his hair away.
It blows the skin from his body.
Soon the bones and flesh are strewn among
particles of sand and mist the wind sends.
Soon his bones are blown to powder
and bones and sand
swirl in the wind.

Only the sound
remains.

Two: Water

All of us, sitting in a park, in rows and rows
and rows of rows and rows. Filling it everywhere.

As far as one can see
rows of beings sit on quiet couches
smiling, aware, awake; cognizant of all the other beings
sitting in rows, resting on couches.

The air is clear, the breeze
vivifying, wafting pleasant vernal smells,
pungent temple smells, or no smells,
just as each requires, sitting as each pleases.

To each as to each is pleasing. The sky
is quiet, shining.
Each is still.
Blissful feelings pass in constant waves across the fold,
rising simultaneously everywhere,
passing from each to the next and quietly subsiding.

◆

Across the vast expanse
a perfect cloud appears —
to each of us it seems to form itself
a distant point above the far horizon —
to each an interesting speck, a salutary blemish,
increasing the perfection of the sky

growing slightly, slowly, showing a perfect shape,
ovoid, ivory white
with delicate puffs and ruffles,
buff, or flush with vermillion, edged in gold.

To each the colors to the pleasure of each.
To each increasing in volume and variety
as each commits attention to its forming.
A gorgeous object poised in the center of the sky,

compelling the sky, controlling the vista for all
and each. The luminous shining dome of perfect turquoise
fringes the clouds. And columns of skylight fan about it.

♦

And now, on the edge of the cloud, a speck or blotch of grey
cloud first appears. It appears as if a doubt
in the eye of one of us, a mote in one of the eyes,
sent to test a doubt.

And soon another of us marks the blemish —
some being off somewhere,
far across the park in another row
assumes the doubt
and knows the speck.

And another blot appears in the luminous cloud face.
And spotted across the field of rows and rows
doubting blots appear across the clouds —
clouds and specks and blots —

to each according to the doubts of each.

The air is clear.
The beings sit in rows.

♦

Now rain falls from the cloud.
Rain falls from the clouds.
The grass is moist.
We sit in rows.
Mist moves in from the sky.
The park is drenched from the downpour.
Little rivulets rush from the park pavillion
meandering rapidly between the sitting rows.
The rain seems more than rain.

Waterfalls crash from pavillions.
Across the shining sky the sea appears.
Enormous, white-crested billows approach from afar.
We sit in rows.
The water rushes at us
loosening the trees
dissolving the knots in the mortar of pavillions.
The roofs come crashing down.
The people sit in their garments, soaked in the overflush.
The trees of the park, uprooted, roll about,
the bark dissolves,
our clothes dissolve.

Now naked rows of persons sit in the flood.
The water lifts up one of us out of the row we have.
And now another — lifted, tossed, deposited
into a maw of waters.

Soon across the fold
waves of water break the seated rows.
Persons tossed in the billows —
the mind of each intent upon the water.
The thoughts of each arush in growing waters.
Soon the limbs of one of us, softened in the deluge,
                              fall into the deluge.
Soon the thoughts of one of us floods the world.
A deluge of rushing memory and intellect
commingling with water-sotted digits, limbs and torsoes.
The thought of water rushing
           fills the scene of water rushing —
vermillion billows roll across the minds —
billowing intellects (flecked with gold and black)
       flash across the flood —
water into water passing —
flux into flux resolved —
chaos swallowed up in its nature —
doubt swallowed up in doubt —

Two thoughts:

Two white signata
sign the Void.

Three: Fire

Dweller in cabins on the outskirts, lush.
Luscious jungle growths enclose.

And on the outskirts of the outskirts,
little fires start up.

The marshals are not concerned.
They continue smoking at their posts.

And now the little houses start to burn.
The paper walls go up on sensate flashes. Quietly
the persons depart and only I myself
am seated
unconcerned.

I am seated on my mat and the sounds of far off fires
begin to reach me. I am not alarmed.

I can hear the susuration, the sizzle, the wings
of birds, the crackling of exotic bark.

I am at ease, at leisure.
There is time as large as the wings of birds
beating above the encampment.
The fires now ring the encampment.
The sounds and cries and rushing
of little groups of mammals reach my ears.
I am unconcerned. I listen
as the roar of conflagration closes round me.

The flames reach far beyond the tallest trees now.

The flames
commute
with the sky. Their momentary turrets pierce the cumuli.
The heat of it rises in huge ballooning canopies.

Waves of it fan across the porches where I linger.
Soon the walls will be aflame. Now the walls
are all aflame.

The searing heat consumes my cubicle. It cannot be endured.
My clothes begin to blaze and the flames
begin to needle me everywhere. I am unconcerned.
Enormous sensations penetrate and consume me.
My belly my hair my skin take flame.
My singed flesh blackens
and bubbles up like pizza crust.

Flames from the end of the Aeon flash about
till flames consume themselves in a single nature.

Then:

Three red signs
shine in the void.

Four: Earth

The earth is still.

You are sitting there
on your little wooden bench
knitting your shoes.

Or using a delicate hammering instrument
to curve the copper object cupped in your hands.

Or talking to friends in the summer afternoon
sitting on long benches
around a wooden table.

A house with a porch and a lawn
upon a street
with other well kept houses — lawns and porches.

You hear a sound on the air, dark and rumbly.
Distant thunder, one of the friends proposes.

You sniff the air for the odor of thunder
but there is no odor.

You watch the upper branches of the maples.
A little breeze. No sense of impending motion.

You sit on the ground.

Or stand.

Or adopt a definitely hunched posture, leaning over the table.

A few old stones lie about the feet of a few old trees.

Some rumbling once again, far to the north
a bit like a herd of mammals from afar.
The sound is a sound approaching —

subtly ominous.
Each wave of approaching rumbling
rumbles closer still.

The intervals of time between the sounds
grow shorter now

and louder sounds overwhelm the softer ones
and larger sounds
supercede the small.

You all are sitting now or standing, no one hunched now.
No one talking or attending the little tasks
upon which each had been, but a few moments earlier,
occupied so intently.

You notice the many little sounds within the larger sounds;
crackling sounds and whistling ones; the noise
of a huge thing, striking the ground with a thud;
the metal parts of intricate machinery
toppling to the floor with a cascade of crackling sounds.

Things are shaking now.
The objects and the table rattle and buzz.
The hammer falls to the ground.
The leaves of the maples are all ablur.
The stones roll over other stones
and set off on a course — then leave that course.

You sit alone. Holding your bench.
The others sit alone.
Or stand.
Holding the beams of the cottage porches for balast.

Things are moving in the air now —
shingles from the slanted rooftops fall from the rooftops
and start upon random courses through the trees.
The shaking of things increases.

The clothes upon your body vibrate oddly.
The seat upon the ground begins to exert
terrible pressure against you. You stand.
Or sit on the ground.

The ground is moving now.

The sounds of falling things ring all about.
An enormous tumult encloses on all sides.
All the buildings are falling down
rising in the air and crashing to the earth.
The earth itself rises up
thrusting boulders into the air.
You can see people everywhere
attempting to assume control of their motion
popping off the earth, falling, scampering,
being thrown across their porches onto the lawns.

The things in flight begin to vibrate uncontrolably.
The outer surfaces are first to fall away.
Then the inward machines disintegrate and scatter.

Shirts are torn from bodies, bodies from themselves.

The sky is a welter of human parts and thing parts
streaming in a vast display.

You yourself are among them.
The thoughts you have
begin to come asunder.

You see your thoughts rattling in the foreground
rapidly becoming other thoughts.
Your memories shake and vibrate — they fly out of you
as you yourself are strewn
across the vast expanse.
You see the thoughts of all things come apart

from each — each person thought and thing
an item in a centerless turbulence without gravitation.

◆

All things grow smaller now.

Everything that can be shaken loose
has been shaken loose.

The parts are as small as they can become.

An infinite dust rains across the void.

The motionless void consumes the dust.

Four black signs remain

at the front of the world.

Five: Space

There really is no
space. The blue
room
resumes the mind.

All of them are gone now.
All of the other creatures — people or whatever.

All of you are gone now

All of me are gone now

into the open space
the mind itself
resumes —

The things of sense relax in their true condition.

The houses relax — the walls
    remaining walls
        give a little —

The furniture responds to the weight of people or things —
the joints relax —
the brittle glue grows moist again

The things of mind relax — all one
blue gust of oxygen, one bottomless
sky. The platforms floating down it —

And on each platform, each of us, sitting absorbedly —

The body of each of us

Blue — absorbed in its nature . . .

Blue the dark

and Blue the work . . .

Two Dreams

the issue of thought in dream.
the stillness of the same.
the ancient mountain.

a car
on a journey going up the dark road.

and later
riding in the car:

a large bird

beating on the roof of it

trying to get inside
or wanting to break the car apart

that there ought not to be
this vehicle, this car
that carries
beings that carry themselves
across the nightland mountains

across the changing of darkness
ever the same

◆

urges that were possible
in the brig of night

unable to move
limbs or thoughts

from across the room

where the night table blackened
and could not be thought

apart from the night

that hovered and consumed

the medium of the earth
sprouting eternal strands and locks
from the skull of stone

the vow to attain the skull
and never sever production

of oils and treasured minerals
from the infinitessimal sockets that dust the bone surface

the thought to exude from the stone until the morning
bring back time itself

and vehicles move again on the open road

Song

an

old

crone

in

to procure

crackers for

her

captured

white

birds

First Message

as much as I am able to degrade my own access and yet trudge
across the most damnably unhappy parking lot of a rosey

flowering
field

      they want to know my name. I withdraw
decisively

parting with the course of my life among the
others and return
to the dimension of forces
operative

Song

. . . someone walks in from the left.

It is a woman of cloths or

a woman of breaths.

She comes down from a certain

height of perspicacity

and delivers

her essence

along with her presence

over to whomever

affected by the words that summon her

                    has produced those words.

She is green and

borne in on

a rush of light, on a pleasant

wind that

freshens your skin as it blossoms

her dress into fresh roughling billows of

the light she is. She takes

your heart

in her mind

and heightens your view.

Second Message

When talking about the highest
matters, don't pull words
from the blue. That is, don't
use sortilege. What then?
In the concentrated light
pulsing in the forehead,
let that light grow hot
white
really be there   loud

a presence that won't let up — won't let you let up.
There in the coin of it.
The maps of being
run through as on a screen . . .

and then resolve in yourself
when the light gives out.

The Tower

In a blizzard of digits   pick the world to wander in . . .

waiting for a new voice to sound
        from very far and
blow "the house" (your house) down
          the house that *you* built
      blown down now   the tower
house of one's own device (or choice) blown

down as a huge

voice

        from "everywhere"

delivers itself
                    of
          such

              speech that the house

of speech you chose, blows

apart and the people
you were

            flash and vanish
          falling

into the black
air

the black
air
of the speech each

of these people
used
blows

into silence
now

and all now
speak

one voice

Entity

Being
      the angry black spider lion demon drawn up
into an abstract potentiality for manifesting as such
                tucked into the gut and its bad
                        digestive apparatus — BAD
because the demon has dissolved itself
          into it *par abstraction*
or you have

dissolved it   created it   abstracted

the natural manifestation of the hairy
      bellied demon spider lion so it withdraws
into an abstraction of its nature

Getting angry and then affectionate in rapid alternation

contradicting people. Being
able to talk to your father and not
being able to talk to
your father

in the same
breath.

The Backhoe

the outrage
of the backhoe
in the back yard

tearing
into the lawn:

the man that drives the backhoe all life long —

a billion insects perish
in the improvement

PEOPLE ARE FISH

or in the river
people who have
recently abandoned
the human state
upon dying deciding
it no longer a safe bet to attain
anything from that
condition of violence —
better be a fish
in a foolish river
rather than

the radio
blasting
after the bastards had long
vanished from the ambience

. . . With five heads they came
to the edge of the beautiful river

and each had a radio and they
cut a trench in the earth
they put the radio
into it, that no one would ever be able to silence
the vicious
noise, the radio
couldn't be terminated . . .

Existence itself is conventional.
The delegates agree
about
   how
     ex-
istence is
to be
distributed
among the constituent
interests in
the field   odd
ideas are cast
aside   blue
gorillas are given
little
share
in existence where-
as the buzz-
ing of vicious engines in
the air, loud talk
and pounding, pounding . . .

A mind

returns

to itself

and says

nothing

        like

a bird

on the shoulders

of a blue gorilla

watching.

Later Poems from "The Sad World"

9. 24. 87

Passing   from one   locality
to another

and passing so by utilizing some
manner of conveyancing — some process.

Being one among
an assortment
of some such beings

and being transformed
by some
manner of transformation
into some
one
other being
among
an assortment
of other such beings.

And coming back again
and being changed back again,
traveling by reverse conveyance —
the car goes backwards
from the town at which
                            one
                  had
          just recently
                      established oneself
back to that town
                from

which
recently one
had departed.

Or turning back into the thing one used to be
    by the backward of the process that
        just recently
            had processed one.

Or turning into oneself —
        remaining
                where one was   but
            taking a conveyance
                for doing so — only
            the conveyance is inoperative,
                            the bus is still.

Or being transformed
by a certain process —
but the process is inoperative:
nothing remains suspended
in a solution of pure water only

and one remains
just as one was
against the process . . .

9. 28. 87

Our town and
            another town
        acrosss a long
                        blank   land.

And journeys
       going
    across that land
      from our town
     to that other.

Our town becomes another one —
across the long, blank land   and
the other town must change
               and be our own.

We have to make a journey
across a long blank land
and come to the other town.

And others from that
distant place must cross
the desert and come
to *our* town.

Part by part and place
       by place.

The locations in our town must become
locations in that other.

But no conveyance may convey these places.

They must change by force
of inward decree alone.

The parts of our town must vanish
and the parts of another town
across an enormous tract
appear where our parts were.

Our parts, our places, our persons and our norms
must
transfer across the earth
to that other town.

The places themselves, I say,
change to other places —

Not only the *things* —
    Not only the ancient houses —
        Not only the earth
        on which those houses
        stand —

But the blank locations
    the rigid laws
    the truths
on which that land was cited — *those* truths
change,
        move,
                become *new*
        truths
                requiring *new*
citations.

And across the barren earth, the blank place
between the towns

another town assumes
what we
assumed.

All the norms we knew
become
the norms that others have.

The Persons switch
down to their personal essences —

not only the bodily parts
that shoot across space
to become the parts of others, now themselves,

but the Living Streams
   the Furrows of Abstract Selfhood
      the Grooves in Time of Dark Concrescent Selfhood

are removed

                    A violence unlike
                       any other violence

                                a little cry goes up

10. 5. 87

Whatever it is
it has
beneath the broken sky
its parts from elsewhere.

And parts from local regions.

And each part sleeps in its passage
along the time of the thing it keeps its house in.

Rocks on the edge of the water
lapping the surface *of* those rocks
and at their inward matters

sending noises of water
across the vacant spaces

And on the other shore
the sounds are reconstructed
by the wardens of incoming noises . . .

That you can be the kind you are and change
        into all the other kinds

That all the other kinds can lose their marks
        and move or change

That the parts combine with the others
in all the ways they can combine
        according to the laws for that

And always
            also
                that things
        can remain as they are
        and that this too
                        is change

10. 26. 87

At whatever moment we choose to inspect the owl
the owl remains
projecting itself
across a continuum of moments.

And the stubbly field
where the lonesome oak remains —
remains.

And every granite stone of it
throws itself
across a continuum of moments.

<u>10. 28. 87</u>

We peel away the cloak of night
and glance at the darkest stone.

It stands in the stubbly field.

We peel away the cloak of night and view
the moment of the oak.

Its bronze leaves shake in the winds.
A shudder of sound ascends.

We peel away the cloak of night
and peer in upon the purchase of white owls.

They clutch the branch.

We peel away the cloak of night and glance
at the moment of ourselves.

The storm has broken a limb from the oak in the night.

<u>11. 3. 87</u>

A little crystal globe
rolls across the moon.

Within its ruby chambers, high enthroned,
a "species creature" contemplates its nature.

And when the waves of moolight sweep across it
the globe will lose its smallness and become
the universal sphere of abstract stone.

The creature will lose its species and become
                                    all of us —

All of us will drift across the moon
in whose waves of light we lose our nature.

In the Sad World waves of moonlight pass across
the strings of precious stones our moments seem.

And the dreams go on
and the changes prosper

11. 6. 87

The elk mind moves its antlers
                flourishing the trees . . .

The little animals huddle in the weather.

11. 11. 87

The little towns — some great metropolis now.
Metropolis 'Ah' —
To it all trucks return. Or can return.
They can be recalled there.

Wherever they travel their cargo
across whatever blank land
to Metropolis 'Ga' or 'Ka'
or some confuted town along the clefts:
from Metropolis 'Ah' a term is set to the movement.

And the elk mind flourishes —

It holds the city 'Ah' in its changing antlers.

And the creatures forget their natures
as they travel
back across the route
to the root metropolis, or from the root metropolis.

They forget their house of mice at Metropolis 'Ah'
traveling the goods to fuel the towns —
forget ancestral towns along the clefts
and the rules they rode to get there
and the owls they used

traveling back to Metropolis 'Ah'
forgetful, longing

Or forgetful, pulsing with the bliss of it.

The town of jeweled pavements
    washed by that white moon

and the jewels transfered (cashiered) in another town —

And the walls of the town, what are they now?
All walk across the line they draw
or pass like mist through open grates —

And the news they travel on conveyances
coming from another town
across degradable spaces:

the news reports the space it passes over.
A voice on the edge of the speech it uses bleeds —
        speech bleeds into not speech —

        grd th t
            k   n s t sh
        d um   uu i

Syntax preserved behind a vigil of negation —

The wardens remain in their booths atop the walls
fielding the trucks.

The universal animals
retract
to the space behind the speech they use,
to the rules before the rules were set,
posting the first generalities.

And the moon wave passes o'er
and the language thickens:

the beasts become ourselves
ensconced in natures.

11. 13. 87

The first generalities — alone
in the broken school
        (broken pavement sumac spumes in air)

People diverse from the analyses that cross them
abuse the thought they find themselves inside of
losing themselves among the thoughts they find
confuting the worlds.

Every beast confutes a different world
and wanders, blissful, desolate

a retract of the apparatus map that spots them
a declension of the beast without a nature
searching for a Door
to get back out or up or into, forth or onward

through the space that marks
the direction of direction

home to Metropolis 'Ah'

        general

             without foundation

Concordance

hides
in the mater

people think
the same way

everyone is an enlightened
one

every stone
unturned

turns
to the north

gathers
green

moss upon its
earthward
stomach

learns
as it turns

and yearns
to turn again

everyone wants
to go home

Agreement then. The things
that all

observe all

do observe

people don't disagree

the whiteness the wonder
the sky

itself —

Ancestors came down
from the stars —

all know that —

we feel it

we can feel the nightsky

twinkling in the background

(the black

ground)

we can hear the ancient music knowledge
working to soothe all woes

woe to him who strays beyond the chord

woe to whomever turns
far from this knowledge

abandoned by the very world he strays
among broken things

the hammer in the dust
the fragile monuments

the causeless linkages between the wounded signs

each is animal enough to drag its members painfully toward the
station of some ancient promised homecoming

the heroes are strewn in the night

but the wars do not occur —
they singe the unreal

there is no "chance" — no loss

regularities march along the void

◆

It grows in intensity in one person's purview but the others remain
stupified, oblivious

thus the cars
run on

the enormous train
rams the barrier

the people
wail

the village
falls

◆

Intensity of thought is like a knife
of light

the rhythm goes forth
from the mind
and stuns community

it takes it all in in a single glance

it lives in the center
of the mountain

◆

The mountain hears and sees, tastes and feels and knows

the mountain weighs each step

a room or hall at the heart of it
contains events each sense domain projects, convenes, recalls

the things of sight are shadowed there

there is a room of sound
where passing throbs and rolling interjections of thunder, white
susuration of waters, cries of beasts
come down

a chamber of odors a tunnel of tastes

the mineral veins and lightless tubules quiver with touch of insect,
mammal, bird

And there are caves of mind whose windows index
 all the other rooms and the doings in them

And over the mountain, up in spaceous air, hung on a bluff
 a little house yet stands . . .

◆

Whatever Is — the little house remains

above the bluff — blue in the morning

when the golden water takes the golden sky —
gold in the evening when the sky grown dark beyond blueness

attends as blue water chills

— Is in a way that neither sense confines nor mind induces

askance

   — aslant

   Attention slides into vacancy

    but remains at attention still

The meanings of the world all hidden else

appear as simple terms —

warm in the generous glance that passes over

    Over the bluff — blue

   and of blue vacancy

     gold

   with the hidden concordance

    of sudden stars

The Hoopoe

1

How much wind
until the earth stop blowing.

You cannot have a reason to make poetry.

These white rocks.

Myself, so far away.

A sheet of lightning, inspecting its own
contingency.

Body, mind. Birds and seals.

The look of the little sea among the rim of mountains.

Why should I tell you?
But that I am not myself until I do.

Trying to work a way among the broken axioms, rattling stones.

2

The machine pursued its own allegiances
and I rode
the great machine
into the weather.

Suddenly a Hoopoe swept out of the north.
It took me up in its beak and claws and feathers
and covered me with the enigmatic breath
of a bottomless oxygen.

What did I know?

My body and my mind
remained below
an oily seal on the violent beaches,
a little bird
in the night
on the broken branches.

My concern was not with these poor animations
but with myself as I slashed along the reaches of the sky
the strange bird screeching as we moved.

Then turn around.
Drop on a rock.

3

Is Being grim or blank?
Does blank consume?
Or is it night?
And if night shelter the little things that produce
the likeness of themselves
in darkness and in strenuous obligation,
what frank mouth is that
that menaces from without
the generous night
to take the mothering night away again
and blanch with sun?

4

Oneself among contingencies. Not
contingency.

Of a piece with the grim machine, the holy mountain.
Complicit with the mouth whose speech emits
the blanks of thought. Standing on a rock.
Confecting thought from that which speech emits
and that matricial atmosphere
whose rocks are thoughts.

5

Late at night.
Sitting in a room
with keys and papers.

No access from this place
to the islands of particularity.

What small seals are.

6

The things in their textures and employments
identities and pock marks, erotic moles
on metonymic flesh
and magical sentiments
charging the speckled rocks

When dawn rains down its dust of welcome,
what lightness up to greet
the brief arousal . . .

7

The mouth a cave of night. A sky of thought.
All space consumed. And time. But earth
with its intimate trajectories, its glistening
discoveries among the larval chaos
its fissures and its grim techtonic slidings
its dry nocturnal inward rocky density

NOT matricial mothering mind of flesh
but gravitational, not implicate of culture, human thought. A rigor
that escapes
that ugly fidgeting thinking thing in selfhood
an essence of crocodile

a tincture of hoopoe fluids

8

not water not air *not* earth not conflux or mixture not number
not mind not force

it is

both thing and thought
co-implicate
singular

9

each item

compounded of the matter it instantiates
and the identity it shrouds

so that the cup of mouth
drink living liquid

10

on every liquid molecule
an image
of a dancing thing
and in that image
the thing itself
present
to itself
and dancing
in itself

11

And I flew away on the Hoopoe's back
and never would return
to the vanishing solidities of our common
dimensionality fantasmal though most firm
in apparency and of the solid
timeless bed rock nature of true mind
— true intimation

12

(I go there
where my true concern both calls and is

in anger
and with grievous laceration
that the things
are feckless in their timid speculations
and will not land
my bird
or give her shelter

They Take the Car Away

They take   the car   away.
They take it away.
They came and took it away.
They came and took the car away.
Took it away.
Took it.
Took the car.
They took my car.
They came and they took my car away.
They came and took my car.
They took my car.

An elephant
triumphant
through the towns.

Large crowds of curious persons.
Stampeding persons. I
on my cabana.
I at the roof
of worlds, roofs
of towns.

I walk, I ride, I rule, I turn away.
I take my elephant away.
Take it from the life of ease
          the life dis-ease
        the animal life of pain.
I take myself away from life of pain —
that white heat shining.

White heat   very fine   and shining
        in the lining
            of the garment
                      that is the world.

The man's bright coat — its secret shining.

Oh he wore it   in the avenue
he wore it
                when it rained
he went to lunch.

They took my car away.
They took my car
away. They took it away.

How can we ever be happy again
How can we be free
How can pleasure
                take us
            home to town

How can we ever be merry again
How can we be gay
Now they have taken my car
Away. They took my car away.

I am an elephant
I have something to say.

I am an elephant
I have something to say.

I have to take my elephant to town
My fine coat shining.

The elephant's gray skin, shining strangely
strangely dull, yet shining
— shining in the rain
    as it walked through town
shining in the mud
    as it wagged and waddled.

Now they have taken my car away
    how can I shine now —

The Hat Rack Tree

Your old hat
sits
on the hat
rack tree
as the plumes
of the tree
grow dry
and wind unravels them.

"No wind is
the King's wind."

Now you go to buy some new
hat. Should it be
just like it?

A new hat sits like a plume
on the hat rack tree.

There is a bird
on that lady's hat —

to pluck its felt?
or shred the brittle veil
that hangs from the brim?

It is a crow
(not my crow).

Something not alive
on the hat rack tree.

What can I see with this?
What can I sell?
Come all comers
to the hat rack tree
and see the lady's hat
with black stuffed crow.

Odd — but the crow's eye lives
with terrible rays
and the feathers shine
with a glint of green —

Wind in the branches
wind in the plumes

strong enough to knock your
hat off. Knock your hats off.

If you were a King
and owned a tree

would you become a crow
with its terrible shining

and charm the wind
into your hat

and wear it
out
to see the world?

A lady's veil
conveys her shining.

She is nervous.

Nor does she gleen
the thing on her hat.

NOTES

"The Lions"

This is an *in memoriam* Lou Kleinsmith, who was my first T'ai Chi Chuan master, in the Cheng Man-ch'ing school.

"Pages from *First Forest*"

These poems are from the concluding section of the first "run" of poems from *The Forest*.

"A Parmenides Machine"

The Parmenides in this piece is more the figure in Plato's late dialogue dealing with Parmenides, than the "Pre-Socratic" author of the fragments attributed to that figure. In this dialogue, the aged philosopher, visiting Athens from Elea, accompanied by his disciple Zeno (of Zeno's Paradox fame) is confronted by a young Socrates and induced, in spite of the fatigues of age, to intitiate him in the mysteries of his philosophic method. This consists in a gruelling series of logical exercises, and it is to these that I refer as a "machine" (though I also confound this machine, perhaps obscurely, with the strange object claimed by authors George Sassoon and Rodney Dale to have been the "Manna Machine" that sustained the Hebrews during the Forty Years and which is reflected in *The Zohar* as "The Ancient One" and "The Ancient of Days" (Cf. *The Kabbala Decoded*, Duckworth, 1978)).

"The Sad Machines"

The sadness is the sadness of the Samsaric world. With this title I make reference to a notion of the intuitionist mathematician and mystical thinker, L.E.J. Brouwer. Brouwer thought that our world has been compromised by our power to construe being in terms of regular numerical series. These series, when correlated with the world in a certain manner, yield what we think of as temporally extended objects and, when correlated in another manner, yield causal chains of events. The construction of such series gives us the capacity to dominate nature technologically but distracts us from our immediate connectedness to both the being of the world and our internal spiritual sources. The world we produce for ourselves with this capacity is "The Sad World."

113

Brouwer thinks that our ability to construct such deleterious series derives from the nature of our intuitions about time, an account of which, as well as excerpts from his writings, are presented in *Io #41, Being = Space x Action: Searches for Freedom of Mind in Mathematics, Art, and Mysticism*, published by North Atlantic Books and edited by myself.

The material at the end of this poem about the "two-headed mammal" is a fanciful imaginalization of Brouwer's time theory and its application to the construction of our number system.

"Later Poems from the Sad World"

"The Sad World," mentioned above, constitutes a "region" of *The Forest* that is dominated by serial or other forms of mathematical order. I have several unfinished pieces that manifest that "region." "Later Poems from 'The Sad World'" makes use of a level of abstraction achieved in the contemporary mathematical discipline known as "Category Theory," an account of which appears in my introduction to *Io 41*.

"The Hoopoe"

The Hoopoe is a figure from the great Persian Sufi Poem, *Mantiq Ut-Tair* (*The Conference of the Birds*) by Farid Ud-Din Attar.

"Concordance"

This is part of a region of *The Forest* called "The Holy Mountain."

"The Tower"

This poem is based on the familiar Tarot card image of a brick tower blasted from above, with male and female figures falling headlong out of it in the ensuing cataclysm.

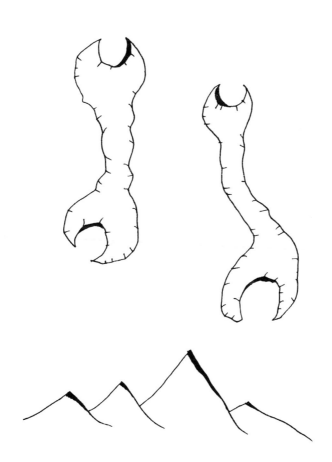

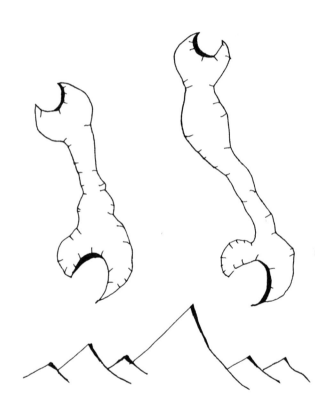

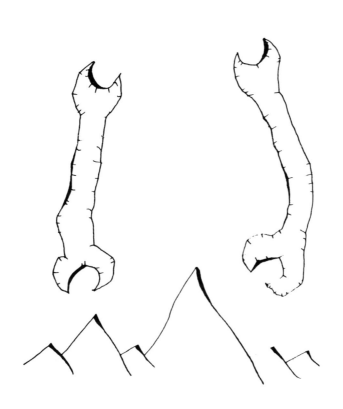

—

About the Author

Charles Stein is the author of nine previous books of poetry including *Parts and Other Parts, Horse Sacrifice,* and *The River Menace,* all published by Station Hill Press. He is the author of the critical study, *The Secret of The Black Chrysanthemum: The Poetic Cosmology of Charles Olson & His Use of the Writings of C.G. Jung,* also from Station Hill, and the editor of *Being = Space × Action: Searches for Freedom of Mind in Mathematics, Art and Mysticism,* published as *Io #41* by North Atlantic Books (1988).

He has collaborated and continues to work with George Quasha in the production of "dialogical" criticism: innovative approaches to the discussion of literature, art, and related concerns. He is the inventor and practitioner of a species of "Sound Poetry," which he has performed with David Arner, George Quasha, Armand Schwerner, and others; he has also performed in works of video-art by Gary Hill and Catherine Schieve. As a member of the Barrytown Orchestra and Music Program Zero's "Composer's Ensemble" (Bard College) he has worked with Benjamin Boretz as an improvisor (clarinet and voice) and contributor of compositions. He has published "Text-Sound Texts" arising from this association in both musical and literary contexts.

He is currently engaged in several on-going projects: the development of ad hoc installations from a collection of objects gathered over a period of thirty years; a philosophical enterprise based on a sustained examination of the early Greek philosopher Parmenides, including a complete translation of the fragments of Parmenides, notes towards which appeared in *Io #41*; other translations of Ancient Greek poetry (including a version of the *Homeric Hymn to Demeter*); a collection of dream writings; work in photography and pen and ink drawing.

He is a Buddhist practitioner in the Dzogchen tradition and has been a student of contemplative disciplines since his youth.

He graduated with a B.A. from Columbia College in 1966 and holds a Ph.D in literature from The University of Connecticut at Storrs. He has taught at SUNY Albany and at Bard College and lives with classical guitarist and choral conductor Megan Hastie in Barrytown, New York where he works as an editor.